OCEAN LIFE UP CLOSE

Emperor Penguins

by Heather Adamson

BELLWETHER MEDIA · MINNEAPOLIS, MN

Note to Librarians, Teachers, and Parents:

Blastoff! Readers are carefully developed by literacy experts and combine standards-based content with developmentally appropriate text.

Level 1 provides the most support through repetition of high-frequency words, light text, predictable sentence patterns, and strong visual support.

Level 2 offers early readers a bit more challenge through varied simple sentences, increased text load, and less repetition of high-frequency words.

Level 3 advances early-fluent readers toward fluency through increased text and concept load, less reliance on visuals, longer sentences, and more literary language.

Level 4 builds reading stamina by providing more text per page, increased use of punctuation, greater variation in sentence patterns, and increasingly challenging vocabulary.

Level 5 encourages children to move from "learning to read" to "reading to learn" by providing even more text, varied writing styles, and less familiar topics.

Whichever book is right for your reader, Blastoff! Readers are the perfect books to build confidence and encourage a love of reading that will last a lifetime!

This edition first published in 2018 by Bellwether Media, Inc.

No part of this publication may be reproduced in whole or in part without written permission of the publisher. For information regarding permission, write to Bellwether Media, Inc., Attention: Permissions Department, 5357 Penn Avenue South, Minneapolis, MN 55419.

Library of Congress Cataloging-in-Publication Data

Names: Adamson, Heather, 1974- author.
Title: Emperor penguins / by Heather Adamson.
Description: Minneapolis, MN : Bellwether Media, Inc., 2018. | Series: Blastoff! Readers. Ocean life up close
 | Audience: Age 5-8. | Audience: Grades K to grade 3. | Includes bibliographical references and index.
 | Description based on print version record and CIP data provided by publisher; resource not viewed.
Identifiers: LCCN 2016052744 (print) | LCCN 2017017258 (ebook) | ISBN 9781626176416 (hardcover : alk.
paper) | ISBN 9781681033716 (ebook)
Subjects: LCSH: Emperor penguin—Juvenile literature.
Classification: LCC QL696.S473 (ebook) | LCC QL696.S473 A33 2018 (print) |
  DDC 598.47–dc23
LC record available at https://lccn.loc.gov/2016052744

Editor: Christina Leighton   Designer: Lois Stanfield

Printed in the United States of America, North Mankato, MN.

Table of Contents

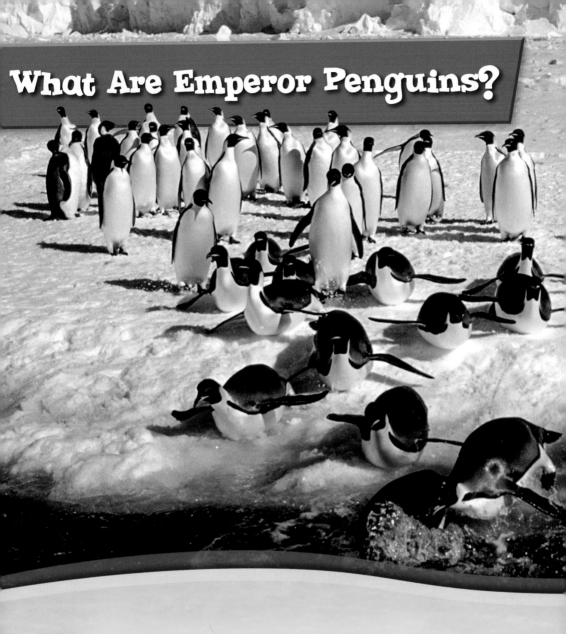

Emperor penguins are the largest penguins in the world. These birds do not fly. They swim in cold, icy water.

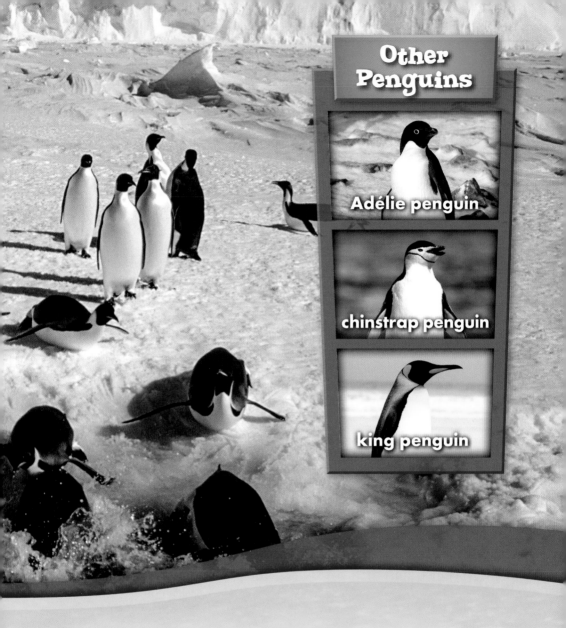

Other
Penguins

Adélie penguin

chinstrap penguin

king penguin

On land, they slide on their bellies. They also **waddle** across the ice.

Emperor penguins are only found in Antarctica. The birds do not have nests or shelter from the snow and wind.

colony

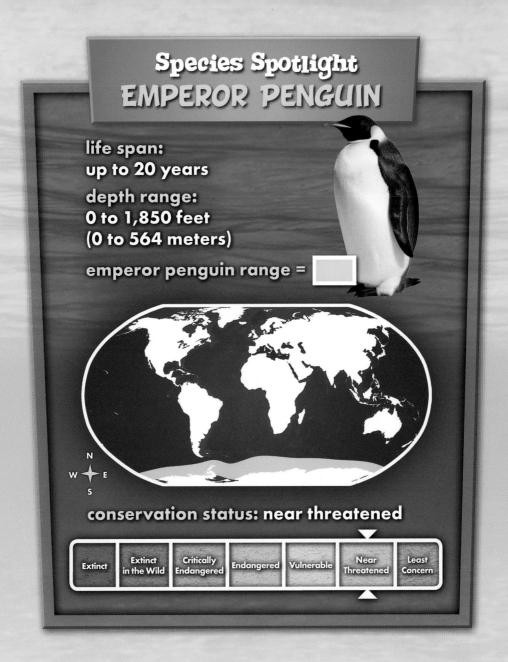

Species Spotlight
EMPEROR PENGUIN

life span:
up to 20 years

depth range:
0 to 1,850 feet
(0 to 564 meters)

emperor penguin range =

N
W + E
S

conservation status: **near threatened**

Extinct	Extinct in the Wild	Critically Endangered	Endangered	Vulnerable	Near Threatened	Least Concern

Instead, they help each other survive. **Colonies** huddle in groups to stay warm.

Black and White

Emperor penguins are black and white with yellow markings around their heads. **Dense** feathers and **blubber** protect the birds from the cold.

8

Identify an Emperor Penguin

long, curved body

yellow markings

wide wings

The claws on their feet **grip** the ice to walk. Their wide wings work as paddles in water.

These penguins stand about 4 feet (1.2 meters) tall. Their bodies are long and curved to help them swim.

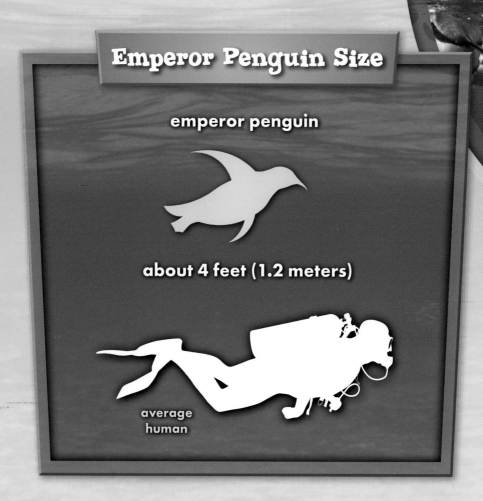

Emperor Penguin Size

emperor penguin

about 4 feet (1.2 meters)

average human

They weigh between 50 and 88 pounds (23 and 40 kilograms).

Deep Sea Divers

Emperor penguins catch krill, squid, and small fish to eat. Sometimes they must travel far to find food.

These **carnivores** dive deep in the water to hunt. They can go as deep as 1,850 feet (564 meters) below the surface!

Catch of the Day

Antarctic krill

Antarctic silverfish

glacial squid

13

Sea Enemies

orcas

leopard seals

Antarctic giant petrels

orcas

Emperor penguins must watch for **predators** when they swim. Seals and orcas hunt them.

Young penguins can be easy **prey** for seals. Large, flying birds may also catch them from above.

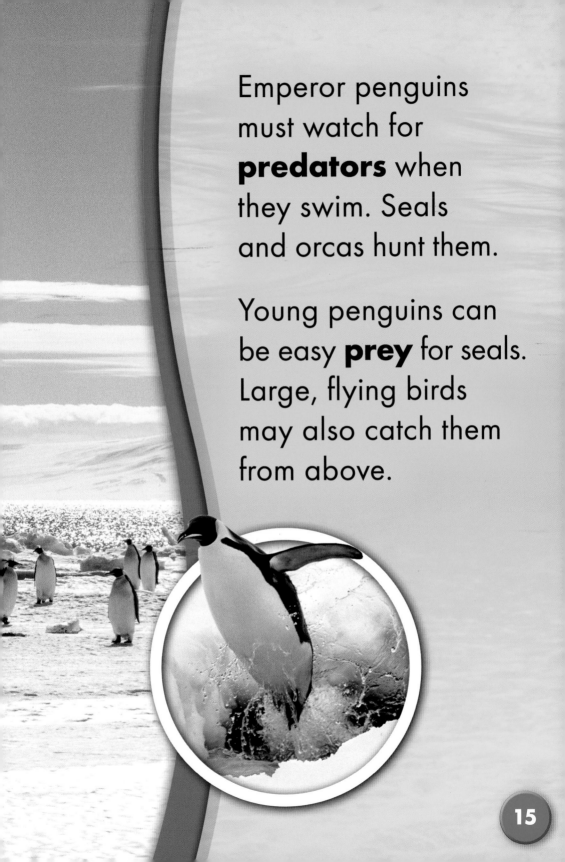

Penguin Families

migrating

Once a year, emperor penguins **migrate** to their **rookeries**. Some walk up to 100 miles (161 kilometers)!

Females and males pair up after the long trip. Soon, females lay one egg each.

egg

Males keep the eggs warm
while the females leave to
find food.

Chicks **hatch** from the eggs two months later. Then the females return to help take care of the chicks.

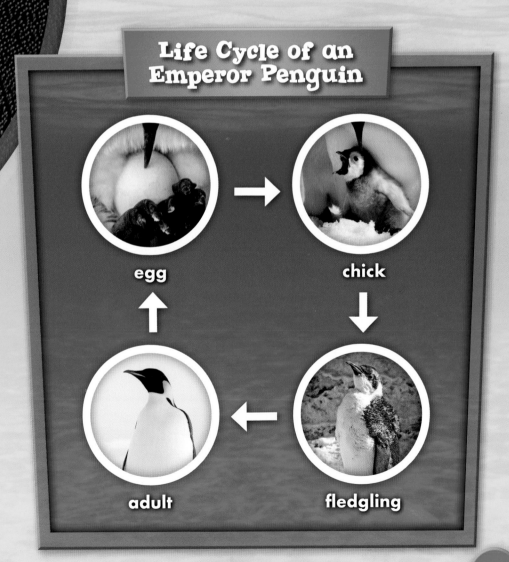

Life Cycle of an Emperor Penguin

egg

chick

adult

fledgling

rookery

Chicks have **downy** feathers. The babies form their own groups to keep warm.

They become **fledglings** after four months. Soon, the young emperor penguins make a trip to the sea!

chicks

Glossary

blubber—the fat of emperor penguins

carnivores—animals that only eat meat

colonies—groups of emperor penguins

dense—thick and very close together

downy—fluffy and soft

fledglings—young emperor penguins that begin to learn to care for themselves

grip—to tightly hold

hatch—to break out of an egg

migrate—to travel from one place to another, often with the seasons

predators—animals that hunt other animals for food

prey—animals that are hunted by other animals for food

rookeries—breeding places for emperor penguins

waddle—to take small steps forward by moving from side to side

To Learn More

AT THE LIBRARY

Cooper, Sharon Katz. *When Penguins Cross the Ice: The Emperor Penguin Migration*. North Mankato, Minn.: Picture Window Books, 2015.

Oachs, Emily Rose. *Antarctica*. Minneapolis, Minn.: Bellwether Media, 2016.

Waxman, Laura Hamilton. *Emperor Penguins: Antarctic Diving Birds*. Minneapolis, Minn.: Lerner Publications, 2016.

ON THE WEB

Learning more about emperor penguins is as easy as 1, 2, 3.

1. Go to www.factsurfer.com.

2. Enter "emperor penguins" into the search box.

3. Click the "Surf" button and you will see a list of related web sites.

With factsurfer.com, finding more information is just a click away.

Index

The images in this book are reproduced through the courtesy of: blickwinkel/ Alamy, front cover (penguin); Nataiki, front cover (background); robertharding/ SuperStock, pp. 2-3 (background), 22-24; Jianhua Liang, p. 3 (penguin); Auscape/ UIG/ Getty Images, pp. 4-5; Dmytro Pylypenko, pp. 5 (top), 13 (left), 14 (center); Ondrej Prosicky, p. 5 (bottom); robert mcgillivray, p. 5 (center); Fred Olivier/ Alamy, p. 6; Jan Martin Will, pp. 7, 9 (bottom); Frank Krahmer/ Exactostock-1672/ SuperStock, p. 8; BMJ, p. 9 (top right); Mario_Hoppmann, p. 9 (top left, top center); Mariia Burachenko, p. 10 (penguin); Paul Nicklen/ Getty Images, pp. 10-11, 12-13; Darren Stevens/ Wikipedia, p. 13 (right); Mim Friday/ Alamy, p. 13 (center); Alexey Seafarer, p. 14 (right); Andrea Izzotti, p. 14 (left); Norbert Wu/ Minden Pictures/ Getty Images, pp. 14-15; Steve Bloom Images, p. 15; Arco Images GmbH/ Alamy, pp. 16-17; Mario_Hoppmann, p. 17; Stefan Christmann/ BIA/ Minden Pictures/ Getty Images, pp. 18-19, 19 (top left); Martin Ruegner/ Exactostock-1672/ SuperStock, p. 19 (bottom left); vladsilver, p. 19 (top right); Sergey Tarasenko, p. 19 (bottom right); Mint Images Limited/ Alamy, p. 20; Jonathan & Angela Scott/ Getty Images, p. 21.